Samuel French Acting Edition

Psycho Night at the Paradise Lounge

by Kitty Burns

SAMUELFRENCH.COM   SAMUELFRENCH.CO.UK

MUSIC USE NOTE

A SPECIAL NOTE TO PRODUCERS

Kitty Burns was asked by a theatre in San Francisco to rewrite *Psycho Night at the Paradise Lounge*, customizing it to the theatre and San Francisco. This was a lot of fun for both the author and producer, and Burns has given her permission to anyone who would like to customize the production to their theatre and city. If you would like help with this, or a fill-in-the-blanks version of the play to use as a template, please contact Kitty Burns through Samuel French.

CHARACTERS

M.C.	Formally dressed
Nick Beasley	Upbeat, slightly nerdy
John Donovan	Stuffy, suit and tie
Sandy Horton	Cute, lively
Cindy Jacobson	Very pretty, dressed formally
Chuck O'Donnley	Good looking, upbeat, self-assured
Alissa Pinkerton	Late 20's, tries in vain to remain calm
Donna Priestly	30's, slightly high-strung
Mike Thompson	30's–40's, serious, subdued
Jackie Sullivan	30's – 40's, prim and proper
Tracie Martilni	20's – Brooklyn accent, lively
Dave Anderson	30's, nervous
Officer Brady	Male, 30's – 40's
Officer Benson	Female, 20's – 30's
Officer Stewart	Male, any age
Office Von Morze	Male, any age

TIME & PLACE

Present day.

San Francisco Bay area.

PSYCHO NIGHT AT THE PARADISE LOUNGE

ACT I

About one minute before the curtain rises, CINDY, who is seated on a stool upstage center, begins singing. ALISSA and DAVE are seated at one table, JOHN and JACKIE at another table with drinks, and TRACIE and DONNA at another with drinks. The waitress, SANDY, is at Dave and Alissa's table taking their order, then exits. Song ends.
CINDY begins singing another song—a Betty Boop type song of the 1940's.

ALISSA. Don't worry, sweetheart. You're doing the right thing. You've got to get her before she gets you.

DAVE. In a way, it's self-defense. I mean, you saw *Fatal Attraction.*

ALISSA. That's right.

DAVE. Although she hasn't exactly done anything harmful yet.

ALISSA. Do you want to wait till she does?

DAVE. No. I'm sick of this. I don't want things to get any uglier than they already are.

ALISSA. Look at it this way. It's pre-self-defense. You're preventing the need for self-defense.

DAVE. Kind of like preventive maintenance or medicine.

ALISSA. Exactly.

DAVE. Do you think she knows we're out in the audience?

ALISSA. Dave, if she knew you were out here, she'd come down off that stool and be kneeling at your feet singing.

DAVE. You're right. I just don't want her to see us.

ALISSA. Don't worry. She can't. Besides, look at her. She never even looks out into the audience. It's like she's singing to herself up there.

DAVE. Yeah. Her eyes look empty, like she's looking inward instead of outward. It's almost spooky.

ALISSA. Speaking of spooky, have you gotten any more love sonnets or gifts in the mail lately?

DAVE. Not since last week. I don't even read them any more or open the packages. I just throw them in the garbage.

ALISSA. You know, I hate to say this, but the sonnets are beautiful.

DAVE. I know. That's the weird part. If they were to someone else or from someone else, they'd be great, but coming from Cindy I hate them. If they were from you, I'd love them.

ALISSA. What if they were from your wife?

DAVE. Don't bring her into this. She's the only innocent one in this whole mess.

ALISSA. I know. I actually feel sorry for her. I'd like to know how you explain all the wrong number phone calls you get from Cindy at night and all the . . .

DAVE. I'd like to know how Cindy keeps getting my new phone numbers. I've had the number changed four times.

ALISSA. How do you explain that to your wife?

DAVE. I don't have to. To a casting director, changing your phone number is like changing your socks.

ALISSA. Well, after tonight you won't have to worry about it anymore.

DAVE. You're right. It'll be a new beginning for us. (*HE takes her hand in his.*) No more harassment, no more presents, no more dreaded phone calls, no more Cindy. And I can finally get back the black boa that Cindy stole from the costume room that night.

ALISSA. Don't remind me of that night.

DAVE. That was long before I knew you.

ALISSA. I know.

DAVE. Besides, I hate thinking of that night myself. If I hadn't been so stupid, none of this would be happening.

ALISSA. You mean if you hadn't been so horny.

DAVE. That too. My wife always says I'll drop my pants at the drop of a hat, and that's exactly what happened. Cindy was helping me put away some costumes and she dropped a French beret, and when she bent over to pick it up, all my vital organs just jump started into gear.

ALISSA. Well, after tonight you'll be able to forget all about it. Are you sure you brought everything?

DAVE. Positive. I went over my check list twice.

ALISSA. Where did you decide to set up the cross-bow?

DAVE. Remember those pictures she sent me when she was trying to talk me into letting her do her one woman cabaret show at the theater?

ALISSA. Yeah?

DAVE. In her letter she described in detail the outfit and accessories she wore for each set, which means that every night at intermission she changes her clothes. So, all I have to do is rig the cross-bow to the wall of her closet so that when she opens the door—Yuk! I don't want to think about it.

ALISSA. It's kind of ironic to think that I was the one who found this cross-bow for you when you directed *Death Trap* and now we're using it for our own little death trap.

DAVE. Yeah. That was the show that brought us together and now it's gonna help keep us together. You know, there's something strangely erotic about actually putting an end to somebody else's life.

ALISSA. I know what you mean. It's wrong, it's sick, and it's the most hideous crime you can commit, and it's making me very excited.

DAVE. Me too!

ALISSA. Are you sure you want to do this?

DAVE. Positive.

ALISSA. Are you prepared to pay the consequences, whatever they might be?

DAVE. Totally.

ALISSA. Are you as turned on as I am?

DAVE. More.

ALISSA. Oh, God, I want you!

(ALISSA and DAVE get up and start walking toward the door and then stop.)

ALISSA. Wait a minute. What are we doing? We have to control ourselves.

DAVE. You're right. We can do this later.

(ALISSA and DAVE go back to their table.)

ALISSA. My God, I just realized something.
DAVE. What's that, babe?

(ALISSA starts to cry.)

DAVE. Alissa, honey, what's wrong?
ALISSA. I'm in love with a murderer! That makes me just as guilty. Oh, God, how did this happen? My last boyfriend was the night manager of a Teddy Bear's Delight ice cream parlor, and now I'm in love with a murderer. My mother was right. I should have stayed in Lakewood and volunteered at our community theater. People in community theater don't get involved in torrid love affairs and kill people they had one-nighters with.
DAVE. You grew up Catholic, didn't you?
ALISSA. Yes.
DAVE. Welcome to the world of the wicked, sweetheart. Now get a grip on yourself. Remember, I'm doing this for us.
ALISSA. You're right. I'm sorry.
DAVE. Let me get this over with.
ALISSA. Good luck, darling. Just be sure nobody sees you going into the dressing room.
DAVE. Don't worry. I'm not about to screw it up. I've waited too long for this. Everything will go perfectly. You'll see. Her dressing room is right next to the men's room. I can easily go from one door to the next.

(Song ends.)

ALISSA. Be careful.

(DAVE gets up and walks off stage right.
CINDY begins singing a comedy-type song of the 1940's.)

JACKIE. That bitch is gonna pay for what she did.
JOHN. You mean to your bitch?

(JACKIE gives him a dirty look.)

JOHN. Sorry.
JACKIE. Look at her sitting up there singing as if she didn't have a care in the world. Well, after tonight, she won't!
JOHN. You're doing the right thing. As your lawyer and as your friend, I back you up one hundred percent. This is not only justifiable revenge for you, but you're doing me a favor too. I am sick and tired of people bringing stupid, idiotic lawsuits into our office. It has to stop somewhere!
JACKIE. Is that all you can think about? My Baby Bumpkins is dead! And all she could say when she killed him was, "You can just go down to the pet store and buy another stupid dog! You don't have to wait to get it repaired. It'll take weeks to repair this car. You can go buy a new dog today." *(Sadly.)* Buy a new dog—like it was a sweater or a hat. You can't just go down to the store and replace the love and affection of a dear, sweet doggie.
JOHN. The insurance company never should have paid for the damage to her car.

JACKIE. What about the damage done to my little baby? Who's gonna pay for that? I'll tell you who—Miss Cindy Jacobson, that's who!

SANDY. (*Enters and comes to John and Jackie's table.*) Can I get you a couple of more White Russians?

JOHN. Yes, please.

SANDY. Right away. (*Exits.*)

JOHN. Why don't you just run over her with your car? Let her see what it feels like.

JACKIE. Don't worry. When she sits at her dressing table and that chandelier comes crashing down on her head, she'll know exactly what it feels like to get squished.

JOHN. Are you sure she won't have her dressing room door locked?

JACKIE. Positive. When I came down here incognito the last two weekends, I checked and the door was unlocked and nobody was watching it. It'll be a cinch to get in.

JOHN. How long will it take you to install everything?

JACKIE. Not long, just a few minutes. All I have to do is hook up a solenoid to the chandelier, and attach the solenoid to a lighter and put a pressure switch on her dressing table chair to release the solenoid. Then when she sits in the chair, three seconds later the lighter will be triggered and light the flame which will burn through the rubber part of the chandelier cord and melt the wax seal on this tube of acid which will drop on the wire of the chandelier. I'll hook a remote control radio transmitter up to a cordless screw driver which is also wired to the solenoid. When the transmitter turns the screw driver, it'll unhook the wires, releasing the chandelier, and splat!

(*Song ends.*)

JOHN. How do you know this is gonna work?

JACKIE. Of course it's gonna work. It worked for the Roadrunner. Wile E. Coyote was flat as a pancake when the chandelier fell on him.

JOHN. OK, as long as you know it's worked before.

JACKIE. Well, it's show time.

(JACKIE exits stage left, passing by Dave as HE comes back and sits with ALISSA. DAVE picks up his glass and then ALISSA picks up hers and THEY click glasses and smile.

CINDY begins singing an upbeat song of the 1960s).

DONNA. God, she hasn't changed a bit since high school. She still has a perfect body, perfect hair, perfect face, perfect voice—She's still Miss Perfect.

TRACIE. You know, I think you got her built up too much in your head. She ain't all that perfect.

DONNA. (*Looks at Cindy inquisitively.*) Yes she is.

SANDY. (*Comes over to Donna and Tracie's table.*) Hi, Ladies! Ready for a refill?

TRACIE. You bet. Another Salty Dog.

DONNA. And another Manhattan—double.

SANDY. Right away. (*Exits stage left.*)

TRACIE. Are you sure you want to do this? This revenge thing—it ain't you. Besides, you know what they say—success is the best revenge.

DONNA. Oh please! Besides, they weren't tormented by Miss Cindy Jacobson all through high school. They didn't have a million zits and a weight problem and some skinny ass priss with perfect skin making up fat names for them—

every month a new fat name. She'd come into the cafeteria when I was eating and get everybody's attention so they could all hear. (*Blows an imaginary trumpet.*) "Attention, everybody! The March, 1975 fat name is Obesity Bong!" Then, that was all I heard for the rest of that month until the next month when I got my new fat name. By the time I graduated, I'd forgotten that my name was really Donna.

TRACIE. Man, what a pisser.

DONNA. My high school years were the worst years of my life—and they're supposed to be the best.

TRACIE. Hey, at least you finished high school. You're one of the richest chicks in the Bay Area. You're the vice president of a hot shot electronics firm, not to mention the fact that you've lost over one hundred pounds, your nose is perfect now, you've gotten rid of that nervous twitch, and you're up to a 36D. Ain't that good enough?

DONNA. No. These improvements cost me a fortune. Why do you think I went through all those years of graduate school?

TRACIE. You're asking me? Me and Mom never could figure that out. But, hey, I ain't knocking it. You're the most literate cousin I got.

DONNA. I had to go through all that school so I could get a good job and get rich so I could afford to make all these changes. Beauty, like most people, can be bought. Between the neurologists, the psychiatrists, and the plastic surgeons, I spent an incredible amount of money, but it was worth every penny.

SANDY. (*Comes back to Donna and Tracie with their drinks.*) OK, that's one Salty Dog and one Manhattan double.

DONNA. Thanks.

SANDY. I'll check back with you later.

(MIKE, CHUCK and NICK enter and sit at a table. MIKE is carrying a brown paper bag.)

TRACIE. Look, why don't you just show this Cindy chick how beautiful you are now. Let her see how great you look. It'd just kill her to see that the dumpy, fat girl she used to make fun of is now drop dead gorgeous, and she'd have all that guilt and regret to live with for the rest of her life.

DONNA. What guilt and regret?

TRACIE. For the way she treated you in high school.

DONNA. Are you kidding? She'd know right away that all this was a result of one surgery after another, and she'd make some crack about my off-the-rack body. No, people like her never change.

TRACIE. Yeah, you got a point there. So where are you gonna put the snake?

DONNA. She changes outfits and jewelry at intermission. There's a coat rack in her dressing room right next to her table with three feather boas on it. She always wears the black boa for her second set. So, I'll just drape Franklin on the same hook with her black boa. She won't be able to see him through the feathers, and by the time she realizes she's picked up a real boa along with hers, it'll be too late, and you know how cranky Franklin can get when he's woken up from a nap—especially when he's hungry.

TRACIE. No shit. How are you gonna get him back after?

DONNA. During all the commotion, I'll just offer to take him to the Humane Society for them. What are they going to do, hold him for questioning? Besides, they'll be so involved with Cindy and so horrified by her untimely death, they won't argue with someone who's not afraid of the culprit. After all, he'll be just as freaked out as everyone else, and I know how to handle him when he's in one of his moods.

TRACIE. I don't think anyone's going to argue with you, you know? I mean, I can't see any of these prisses in here touching a boa constrictor.

(Song ends.)

DONNA. Oh, God! Look at this. She makes me so sick! Every time she finishes a song, she tosses her hair back and strikes a pose. *(Imitates Cindy.)* I'm doing the world a favor by getting rid of her. *(Strokes the side of her purse and says to it.)* Come on, baby, you've got a job to do. *(Picks up her purse and exits stage left passing by JACKIE who enters and sits with John.)*

ALISSA. Did anybody see you?

DAVE. No. It went perfectly. You didn't hear anything out here did you?

ALISSA. Over that? *(Points to Cindy.)* No. Her screeching covered up any noise you were making.

(CINDY begins singing a show tune. SANDY enters from stage right and goes to Mike, Chuck and Nick's table.)

SANDY. Hey, Mike! How you doing?

MIKE. (*Gets up and hugs Sandy.*) Great. How about you?

SANDY. Pretty good. I sure miss you, though. I can't stand listening to her every night. Oh well, as soon as she finishes getting everything she wants out of Rob, she'll probably quit anyway. But then, I don't know. She does have it pretty cushy here. Oh well, what can I get you guys tonight?

CHUCK. I'll have a beer—anything on tap.

NICK. Scotch—rocks.

MIKE. I'll have . . .

SANDY. Rum and Coke.

MIKE. You got it.

SANDY. I'll be right back. (*Exits stage right.*)

CHUCK. (*Looking up at Cindy.*) Are you sure you want to put that body out of commission?

MIKE. It is a shame, isn't it? You know, she was almost worth it. She is one of the best I've ever had. I'll give her that. In a way, it's my own fault. I never should have introduced her to Rob. I should have known she'd sleep with him. She'll screw anyone who can help her career. That's why she screwed me—just to get to Rob. She told me once she'd do anything to get a position in a nightclub like this.

CHUCK. I wonder which position got her this position.

MIKE. After tonight she'll only be in one position—on her back permanently. And her tombstone will read:

You got where you are by being such a slut,

Though you were one hell of a screw.

I hope that the end justifies the means.

And Cindy, was it good for you?

CHUCK. Just let me have one shot at her first.

MIKE. No! I have to do this tonight. With Rob and Heidi on vacation, the only ones here who know me are the waitress and the cleaning lady, and now that I'm not performing here any more, the cleaning lady doesn't come in until the show's almost over, and we'll be long gone by then.

CHUCK. What about the waitress?

MIKE. Sandy's cool. She's my buddy. Besides, she hates Cindy just as much as I do, especially for screwing her way into my job. Sandy loved my act. (*Thinks to himself and laughs.*) You know, she actually said to me once, "I love that little jack-in-the-box of yours. It's so funny when he pops up just at the right times. He's a killer!"

NICK. Out of the mouths of babes.

MIKE. Yeah. She had no idea she was making a prophecy. But then, neither did I at the time.

CHUCK. How do you know Cindy will turn the crank when she sees it on her dressing table?

MIKE. She was once one of Jack's biggest fans. Don't worry. She'll crank him open. Are you sure you put enough of that stuff in there?

NICK. There's enough gas in there to take out Godzilla.

MIKE. As long as it doesn't just knock her out.

NICK. Hey, you hired me to do a job. I've been a chemist long enough to know how much gas I need for a lethal dose.

SANDY. (*Enters with drinks for Mike's table.*) Here you go, guys. That's one beer, one scotch rocks, and one rum and coke.

MIKE. Thanks, Sandy. We're gonna run a tab, OK?

SANDY. Great! See you in a bit. (*Exits.*)

MIKE. Here's to the sweet smell of revenge. (*MIKE, CHUCK, and NICK click glasses.*) God, look at that slut. Take away the body, the face, the hair, and the voice and what have you got?

CHUCK. Give me an hour with her and I'll let you know.

MIKE. All right, granted, she's definitely great to look at, but that's it. Besides, she knows it. She's so in love with herself. She doesn't even play to the audience. Look at her. She looks bored, lifeless.

CHUCK. Which she soon will be.

NICK. Yeah. (*Mimics shooting Cindy.*) She's one dead singer.

CHUCK. (*In a British accent.*) She's not dead. She's resting.

NICK. (*In a British accent.*) She is dead. She's bleeding demised. She's passed on. This singer is no more.

CHUCK AND NICK. This is an ex-singer.

MIKE. Would you assholes knock it off? I'm sweating bullets over here and you're making jokes. I mean I'm really taking a risk here tonight. Everybody's going to know who did it. Jack Attack has been my side-kick for years and everybody here knows him. And even if by some major miracle I do manage to pull this off without getting caught, I'll never be able to use Jack again. The way you had to rig the gas in there, I'm afraid it's gonna do him in as well as Cindy.

NICK. Yeah, but what a way to go. You said Jack Attack was famous for his sarcasm and insults. Well, this will be Jack's monumental attack, his finest hour, his grand finale.

CHUCK. Man, I hope this is worth it to you. If you get caught, you'll be in for twenty years.

MIKE. Wait a minute. Are you forgetting someone? Your friend, Nick, got the gas and put it in there for me, remember?

CHUCK. That's right. We're all in this together.

MIKE. Why you? You didn't do anything. I don't even know you.

CHUCK. Hey, I can be an accomplice if I want to. Why should I get left out?

NICK. That's right. He's with me. So like he said, we're all in this together.

MIKE. God damn it! Why does she still turn me on?

CHUCK. Great legs, great ass, great tits, great hair.

MIKE. That must be it.

CHUCK. You'd better hurry, man. If her sets are thirty minutes, you don't have much time.

MIKE. Yeah, you're right. OK, Cindy, and now for something completely different.

(MIKE picks up his bag and exits stage left, passing Donna as SHE enters and returns to her seat.)

TRACIE. So, how'd it go?

DONNA. He's resting comfortably. God, I wish I could be there to see this!

TRACIE. You know, that's a very good point. Maybe we should get out of here.

DONNA. Are you kidding? And miss the announcement that the second half of the show has been cancelled? No way! Besides, I want to get Franklin back.

TRACIE. Oh yeah, that's right. OK.

SANDY. (*Enters and goes to Tracie and Donna's table.*) How're you ladies doing?

DONNA. Just who I wanted to see. I'll have another.

SANDY. Double?

DONNA. Double.

TRACIE. (*To Sandy.*) Make that a single.

DONNA. Chill out. (*To Sandy.*) Double.

TRACIE. Single. We're going to be here a while, remember?

DONNA. OK, OK.

TRACIE. I'll have another, too.

SANDY. OK, so that's one Salty Dog and one Manhattan—single.

DONNA. Right.

(*SANDY starts to walk away. DONNA tugs on Sandy's skirt.*)

DONNA. Bring two.

(*SANDY laughs and exits stage right.*)

TRACIE. Hey, come on. If you want to stick around here, you better cool it. They're gonna call the cops as soon as they find her, you know, and they're going to question everyone in the place, and when you talk to the cops, you got to be real careful. You could blab yourself right into jail.

DONNA. I'm just getting a little head start on celebrating, that's all.

TRACIE. Yeah, and I know how you get when you celebrate. You're gonna end up bragging to the whole bar about what you did and end up behind bars.

(*Song ends.*)

DONNA. You're right. I can't get drunk. I want to be completely aware of what's going on. I want to remember every minute of this night. There'll be plenty of time to celebrate later. For now I'll just say . . .

(*EVERYONE at each table raises their glass and says together:*)

ALL. Good-bye, Cindy.

(*CINDY begins singing a ballad. SANDY goes to Dave and Alissa's table.*)

SANDY. Are you ready for another?
DAVE. I know I am.
ALISSA. Me too.
SANDY. (*Takes their glasses from the table.*) OK, be right back. (*Exits.*)
DAVE. This waiting is driving me crazy. When is intermission? This set has to be over soon. I can't stand it anymore. I have to get up and walk around. (*Starts to get up.*)
ALISSA. Sit down, Dave. You don't want to draw attention to yourself.
DAVE. You're right. (*Starts tapping his fingers on the table.*)

ALISSA. (*Puts her hand over his to stop the tapping.*) David? (*Pause.*) Tell me about your new production, David. How are rehearsals going?

DAVE. (*Looking nervously at Cindy.*) They're alright.

ALISSA. (*Turns Dave's face so HE's looking directly at her instead of at Cindy.*) How is the new stage manager working out?

DAVE. He's fine. He's good. (*Starts to calm down.*) Yeah, yeah, he really is. He's very good. He's already got all the props organized and typed up cue sheets for lights and sound. Actually the guy's great. If I had to lose you as a stage manager, I couldn't have asked for a better replacement.

ALISSA. I'm so glad. It was a hard decision for me to make, but when we started planning what we did tonight, I knew it would be better if we weren't working together.

DAVE. But with all the talk about murder in the new play, what if it starts to get to me and I need to talk to you. You won't be there for me.

ALISSA. I'll always be there for you. If you need me, you just call and I'll come right over. You're not alone and you never will be.

DAVE. Thank God I have you.

JACKIE. When is she gonna finish that howling?

JOHN. Don't worry. Intermission has to be soon.

JACKIE. I just want this to be over with.

JOHN. So do I. We both have a lot at stake here tonight.

JACKIE. You said I was doing the right thing.

JOHN. And you are. This had to be done. Even the Bible says, "An eye for an eye."

JACKIE. That's right. People have to stop getting away with murder. Of course, what I did isn't murder. This is justifiable revenge, like Noah's flood, or the destruction of Sodom and Gomorrah, or turning Lot's wife into a pillar of salt. Sometimes revenge is good. I mean, if God did it, it must be OK, right?

JOHN. Right.

(SANDY enters and delivers Dave and Alissa's drinks.)

JACKIE. So how come I feel like a bolt of lightening is gonna strike me any minute?

JOHN. Because, unlike Miss Cindy, you have a conscience.

JACKIE. Yeah, I do, don't I?

JOHN. That's right. And if anything goes wrong, you've also got your lawyer present.

JACKIE. John, you're an auto claims lawyer. Besides, what do you mean, if anything goes wrong?

JOHN. Relax. Nothing is going to go wrong. You didn't get caught installing all that stuff, and you wore gloves so they can't get finger prints, so you have nothing to worry about.

(JACKIE looks down at her hands which don't have gloves on them.)

JOHN. I mean, look at you. who would even think that you would know what a solenoid is much less know how to install one and make it work?

JACKIE. What's that supposed to mean? Do you think I look stupid?

JOHN. No! All I meant was that you don't look like the mechanical type all dressed up like that.

JACKIE. John?

JOHN. Yes?

JACKIE. Don't panic.

JOHN. What do you mean, don't panic?

JACKIE. I forgot my gloves.

JOHN. What? How could you forget your gloves? You remembered all that mechanical stuff and you forgot your gloves?

JACKIE. I'm sorry, but I had a lot on my mind. I mean, if I had forgotten anything, left any small part out, the whole thing wouldn't have worked. Every detail was so important. I'm lucky I only forgot my gloves. What am I going to do?

JOHN. You've got to get back in there and wipe off your finger prints.

JACKIE. I can't go back in there. Intermission is going to be any minute.

JOHN. Then do it after intermission.

JACKIE. After her little accident? How am I going to get in there?

JOHN. That's right. They're not going to let you into her dressing room after she's been murdered.

JACKIE. Wait a minute. I'm wearing white. I'll tell them I'm a nurse!

JOHN. Perfect.

SANDY. (*Enters and goes to Alissa's and Dave's table.*) Are we ready for another round here?

DAVE. We sure are.

SANDY. OK, two more Colorado Bulldogs coming right up. (*Exits stage right.*)

ALISSA. Can you get a pitcher of Colorado Bulldogs?

DAVE. In this place I bet you could get a pitcher of anything.

(Song ends.
MC enters.)

M.C. Ladies and gentlemen, Cindy is going to take a short break, but she'll be back in a few minutes, so don't go away.

(CINDY exits stage left. EVERYBODY sits quietly looking at each other nervously. Suddenly, offstage left there is a SCREAM and a lot of CRASHING and BANGING noises.)

END OF ACT I

ACT II

CHARACTERS are just as they were at the close of Act I.

M.C. Ladies and gentlemen, due to circumstances beyond our control, the second half of tonight's show will have to be cancelled. We would like to request that everyone please remain seated. Of course, if you need to use the rest room, you may do so, but please return to your table as quickly as possible and do not leave the lounge area.

ALISSA. (*To M.C.*) What happened?

M.C. Nothing for anyone to be concerned about at this time.

JOHN. How long do we have to stay here?

M.C. Not long. You'll all be able to leave soon.

(A police SIREN is heard offstage.)

NICK. Oh God, it's the cops.

DONNA. I feel sick.

TRACIE. Do you think having the equivalent of five Manhattans in the last hour could have anything to do with that?

DONNA. No. Believe it or not, I feel stone cold sober, but sick.

TRACIE. What then? Are you starting to regret what you did?

DONNA. Not a bit. I just don't want to get caught.

TRACIE. It's just nerves. You'll feel better when you get Franklin back and we get out of here.

DONNA. Thank you, Dr. Joyce Brothers.

DAVE. You know, now that it's over and done with, I don't feel as turned on by this as I did before.

ALISSA. Me neither.

DAVE. I'm not sorry I did it, but just the thought of even possibly going to jail is turning my stomach.

ALISSA. You're not going to throw up, are you?

DAVE. No, it's not that bad.

ALISSA. Good. You don't want to draw attention to yourself.

DAVE. Yeah, right. (*Sickly.*) Oh, God!

ALISSA. Just take a deep breath through your nose and let it out slowly through your mouth.

(HE does.)

ALISSA. Again.

(HE does.)

ALISSA. Better?

DAVE. A little.

(A POLICEMAN enters from stage right with a partially eaten donut in his hand and addresses the people.)

OFFICER BRADY. Ladies and gentlemen, my name is Officer Brady. Please don't be alarmed, but my partner and I are here to conduct an investigation, and will need everybody's full cooperation. For now, we ask that you restrict yourselves to the lounge area and rest rooms only. We will begin our investigation in the office (*Points offstage right.*), so just talk among yourselves until we return. (*OFFICER BRADY exits stage right.*)

JOHN. You've got to get in there and wipe off your fingerprints.

JACKIE. I know.

JOHN. Don't forget, there are two cops in there thinking up a shit-load of questions to ask us.

JACKIE. Oh, God! What are they going to ask?

JOHN. Probably just the typical stuff. Did anybody hear or see anything suspicious? Is there a mechanical genius in the house?

JACKIE. Very funny.

JOHN. Well, I don't know what they're going to ask. I only know auto claims questions.

JACKIE. I need another drink.

JOHN. Relax! Just get in there, grab a blouse or something out of her closet, use it to wipe off your fingerprints, and get the hell out of there.

JACKIE. OK. I'd better go now while the coast is clear. (*JACKIE exits stage left.*)

DAVE. If I'm going to get the cross bow and that black boa back, I'd better do it now while they're in the office.

ALISSA. Forget the boa.

DAVE. No way. I'm directing *Mame* next season, and I'll need it. Anyway, she stole it from us. It belongs to the theater. Besides, Cindy isn't going to need it anymore.

ALISSA. That's true, but you'd better wait. I saw someone go out to the ladies room a minute ago.

DAVE. That's OK. I'll just pretend I'm going to the men's room again. It worked the first time.

(The sound of an ARROW being shot and a GASP is heard offstage.)

ALISSA. I just think you should be extra careful now with the police here.

DAVE. I will be.

(JACKIE is seen offstage right staggering with an arrow sticking out of her chest. SHE falls [unnoticed] in the exit going from the stage to the rest rooms.)

ALISSA. You were right. Everything went perfectly. Let's just keep it that way.

DAVE. This won't take long. Order me another drink, and I'll slip into the dressing room, throw the boa around my neck, grab the cross-bow, and I'll be back before my drink gets here.

ALISSA. Be sure to pull the collar of your coat up after you put that thing on. You'd look slightly suspicious coming back from the rest room wearing a black boa. I know you're in show business, but that's pushing it, even for a director.

DAVE. I'll be right back. *(DAVE walks to the exit leading to the rest rooms. HE sees Jackie's body lying on the floor, looks around inquisitively, and carefully steps over her body and goes into the dressing room.)*

DONNA. I wonder how Franklin's doing?

TRACIE. Franklin? Aren't you just a little bit curious as to how Cindy is doing, huh?

DONNA. I know how Cindy is doing. She's dead.

TRACIE. So what if Franklin wandered off somewhere?

DONNA. No, I'm sure this experience has sent his blood pressure sky high, and when he gets upset he just curls up in a ball and lies perfectly still. It'll be very easy to slip him back into my purse.

(DAVE is seen offstage right with a black feather boa around his neck, clutching at his throat as if HE's struggling to pull something away. HE fights for a while and then falls [unnoticed] on top of Jackie's body.)

TRACIE. What if he's still upset and won't let you pick him up? Huh? What then? Remember how weird he got when he squeezed the stuffing out of that big toy mouse you gave him for his birthday?
DONNA. I know his favorite accupressure points. I'll get him to relax. Once he calms down, he'll be just fine, but we'll have to feed him as soon as we get home tonight.
TRACIE. You'll have to feed him as soon as we get home tonight. I'm not going near him. It's going to take him a week to unwind from this.
DONNA. No it won't. He'll be fine. He was OK in a couple of hours after the mouse incident.
TRACIE. Donna, that was a pink and white stuffed mouse with a bow in it's hair and one-and-a-half-inch eyelashes! Cindy was a living, breathing human being! There's a big difference.
DONNA. Not to Franklin. If he can't eat it, he doesn't care what it is. Don't be so dramatic. He'll be slithering around the house tonight like nothing happened.
TRACIE. I hope you're right.
DONNA. I'd better go get him.

TRACIE. Hey, while you're in there, check out her dressing table. Maybe some of that jewelry she has is real.

DONNA. Great idea!

TRACIE. I'm only kidding, you moron! Just grab Franklin and get the hell out of there.

DONNA. OK—Well, maybe I'll take a quick look around and see what she's got. Be right back.

(DONNA walks to the exit leading to the rest rooms. SHE sees Jackie and Dave's bodies and stops, looks around nervously, and then carefully steps over the bodies and enters the dressing room.)

NICK. Maybe you should go get Jack out of there. It's stupid to leave evidence laying around.

CHUCK. Yeah, the cops probably won't be out for a while. I bet you've got time.

MIKE. I've been thinking the same thing. They didn't say anything about him before, so maybe they didn't see him in there. If they did, they probably would have arrested me right away.

NICK. Cindy might have knocked him off the table when she keeled over.

CHUCK. Yeah, she's probably down on the floor all sprawled out, just lying there.

NICK. Waiting for you.

MIKE. Man, you guys are sick!

CHUCK. We may be sick, but Cindy is dead!

NICK. Yeah. Mission accomplished.

MIKE. It was kind of weird going into my old dressing room again, especially looking at the way Rob remodeled it for her. The only thing that's the same is the dressing table. God, that dressing room was like a sanctuary to me. Every time I walked in there it was like I was in my own world—no problems, no bills, no women out to get my job—just me and Jack. Right before I went on stage, I used to hold him up next to me and look at ourselves in the mirror and say to him, "OK, Buddy, let's go kick some butt."

(Offstage is heard, "Pop Goes the Weasel" as if from a jack-in-the-box.)

CHUCK. I have a feeling they're going to have an opening for a new act here very soon. Maybe you can get your job and your dressing room back.

MIKE. Yeah, right. Then when the next slut comes along, I'll be out of work again. No thanks. But I do miss everybody here.

NICK. You said you worked here for two years, and Sandy sure seems to miss you, and if everyone else does too, your boss would probably give you your old job back.

(DONNA is seen offstage right holding a jack-in-the-box trying to close it, and falling [unnoticed] on top of Jackie and Dave's bodies.)

MIKE. Without Jack?

NICK. Go get him. I'll take him home tonight and try to fix him.

MIKE. I don't know. I'm not sure it's worth the trouble.

CHUCK. Maybe you just need a little reminder of the good old days. When you go in to get Jack, sit at the dressing table and look in the mirror at you and Jack together like you used to do before each show. You'll get that old feeling back and be dying to talk to Rob about working here again.

MIKE. Yeah, maybe you're right. It would be great to sit at my old table again. Maybe it'll trigger something.

NICK. Sure it will. Now hurry up before the cops come out.

(MIKE gets up and walks to the stage left exit. HE sees the three bodies and stops. HE looks around nervously, backs up, and takes a running leap over the bodies and goes into the dressing room.
OFFICER BRADY enters from stage right.)

OFFICER BRADY. Ladies and gentlemen, first of all, I want to thank you for your patience. It looks as though some of you may be in the rest rooms, so while we're waiting for them to return, I'd like to fill you in on why you've been detained. We have been called in to conduct an investigation. The case has been solved, and you are all free to . . .

(Offstage, from the dressing room, is heard a SIZZLE, a SCREAM, and a loud CRASH. EVERYONE jumps out of their chairs nervously.)

CHUCK. Mike?!

OFFICER BRADY. What the hell was that? Everybody stay where you are.

(EVERYONE sits down as OFFICER BRADY walks over to the exit leading to the rest rooms. HE stops when HE see the three bodies.)

OFFICER BRADY. What is this? Where did these come from?

(CHUCK starts to get up.)

OFFICER BRADY. Stay where you are. Everybody just stay right where you are. *(Yells to the office.)* Officer Stewart, get in here!

(OFFICER STEWART enters from stage right with the M.C.)

OFFICER STEWART. What's been going on out here? Who are these people?
OFFICER BRADY. They were sitting at tables with these people when we came in. Don't ask me how this happened. Just get homicide down here right away.

(OFFICER STEWART exits stage right to the office.)

OFFICER BRADY. *(To people at tables.)* All right, let's do this as calmly as possible. *(To M.C.)* You just stand over there till I need you. Now, I want all of you to form a line, single file and one by one come up here, and without touching anything, I want you to identify these people.

(EVERYBODY gets up and forms a line. TRACIE first, JOHN second, ALISSA third, CHUCK fourth, and NICK last.
OFFICER STEWART enters.)

OFFICER BRADY. *(To Officer Stewart.)* You go check out that crash in the other room.

(OFFICER STEWART exits stage left to Cindy's dressing room, jumping over the bodies.)

OFFICER BRADY. OK, you first. You know anyone here? *(Points to the bodies.)*
TRACIE. *(Walks over to the pile of bodies.)* Oh, my God! That's Donna!
OFFICER BRADY. Donna who?
TRACIE. My cousin, Donna Priestly.
OFFICER BRADY. Stay back. Don't touch anything.
TRACIE. But that's my cousin.
OFFICER BRADY. I'm sorry, but I'm going to have to ask you to please go back to your table. Next?
JOHN. *(Walks over to the bodies.)* This one here is my client.
OFFICER BRADY. Her name please?
JOHN. Jackie Sullivan.
OFFICER BRADY. Thank you. Please go sit down. Next?
ALISSA. *(Walks over to the bodies. Hysterical.)* Dave! Oh, God, no. David, what happened?
OFFICER BRADY. Ma'am you're going to have to compose yourself. Come on over here and sit down. *(Helps her back to her table.)* What is Dave's last name?

ALISSA. Anderson.

OFFICER STEWART. (*Enters from dressing room.*) There's another body in the dressing room.

CHUCK. Where's Mike?

OFFICER BRADY. Who's Mike?

NICK. The guy we came in with.

OFFICER BRADY. Maybe he's in the bathroom.

NICK. Was the body in the dressing room a man or a woman?

OFFICER STEWART. A man.

CHUCK. Long brown hair, wearing jeans and a black leather jacket?

OFFICER STEWART. That's right.

NICK. That's Mike.

OFFICER BRADY. Go sit down.

(*CHUCK and NICK sit at their table.*)

OFFICER BRADY. Who wants to tell me what happened here?

(*Nobody says anything.*)

OFFICER BRADY. Hey, come on. Some of you may be witnesses to these crimes, assuming these people didn't die of natural causes. You have nothing to be afraid of by talking to us—unless you're more than just witnesses to the crimes.

JOHN. I didn't kill anybody. I haven't left the room all night.

EVERYONE. Me neither.

NICK. We've been out here all night too.

TRACIE. Hey, what about the staff?

OFFICER STEWART. They're being questioned now.

TRACIE. What for? Yous two got radar or something? These people weren't dead when you came in here. What were you questioning people for?

OFFICER STEWART. We came here to investigate a series of robberies.

NICK. At the Lounge?

OFFICER BRADY. That's right. Things have been disappearing from here for the last six months. That's what we came down to investigate.

OFFICER STEWART. Let's get back to these dead people over here. They must have something in common.

OFFICER BRADY. Do any of you know each other?

EVERYONE. No.

OFFICER BRADY. To the best of your knowledge, did the dead people know each other?

JOHN. I don't think so. We've been sitting here in the same room together, and nobody seemed to recognize each other.

OFFICER BRADY. (*To Officer Stewart.*) What's the connection? There has to be some common ground here. If they didn't know each other . . .

CHUCK. Maybe there is no connection. Maybe they all got food poisoning tonight wherever they ate dinner.

OFFICER BRADY. Hey, you're the witnesses, they're the dead people, and we're the police. We will figure this out.

CHUCK. Just trying to help.

(OFFICER STEWART enters from stage right.)

OFFICER BRADY. Officer Stewart, what was that crash we heard where you found the fourth body?

OFFICER STEWART. It was the damndest thing. This guy was sitting at the dressing table, and the chandelier fell down on his head.

JOHN. It worked!

OFFICER BRADY. What worked?

JOHN. Nothing.

OFFICER BRADY. If you know something about what's happened here, you'd better tell us.

JOHN. No. I have no idea what happened. I was just thinking about something else.

OFFICER BRADY. (*To Chuck and Nick.*) I have a few questions for you two. What was your friend, Mike, doing in the singer's dressing room?

CHUCK. He's not our friend. We sort of worked for him.

NICK. (*Hits Chuck.*) Mike used to work here. He just went in to look around and sit at his old dressing table one more time—you know, for old time's sake.

OFFICER BRADY. So then, this singer replaced him?

NICK. (*Upset.*) That's right. He was replaced by Cindy Jacobson.

OFFICER BRADY. Why do you say it like that?

NICK. She was flat.

CHUCK. Not from where I was sitting.

OFFICER BRADY. *Did Mike know her?*

CHUCK. I don't know. He might have.

NICK. (*Hits Chuck.*) No, he didn't. She worked here after he did.

CHUCK. That's right. I forgot.

OFFICER BRADY. Why did he leave?

NICK. Hey, what is this? You're questioning us like Mike is a suspect or something. Mike's dead, remember?

OFFICER BRADY. Precisely. He was killed in Cindy's dressing room, which makes me believe that Cindy was the intended victim.

CHUCK. How do you know it wasn't an accident?

OFFICER BRADY. Since there was no earthquake tonight and this is a relatively new building, my guess is that the chandelier has been tampered with. Not to mention the fact that there are also three other dead bodies right outside her dressing room door. Which brings me back to the assumption that there is some connection between these four dead people. Officer Stewart, I want you to check around the bodies and see if you can find anything that may have been a murder weapon.

(OFFICER STEWART puts on rubber gloves and goes over to the bodies and being careful not to disrupt the crime scene, looks at each one.)

OFFICER STEWART. What in the world? Look at this! What in the hell went on out here?

OFFICER BRADY. *(Goes over to the bodies.)* Our murder weapons are some kind of bow and arrow, a chandelier, and a jack-in-the-box? *(Puts on rubber gloves and picks up the jack-in-the-box.)* A jack-in-the-box that smells like gas? *(Puts the jack-in-the-box down on the floor next to the bodies.)*

OFFICER STEWART. What about this guy? Don't tell me he was killed by a feather boa?

TRACIE. Franklin!

OFFICER STEWART. His name is Franklin?

TRACIE. No. I don't know him.

OFFICER STEWART. Then who's Franklin?

TRACIE. Nobody. I was just thinking out loud.

OFFICER STEWART. Would you people stop thinking out loud! Was this guy wearing a feather boa when he came in here tonight?

NICK. No way. I definitely would have noticed that.

M.C. Let me see that. (*Looks at boa.*) That's Cindy's boa.

OFFICER BRADY. Are you sure?

M.C. Sure I'm sure. She always wore her black boa with silver sparkles on it for the second half of her show. Let me check her dressing room and see if hers is there.

OFFICER BRADY. Officer Stewart, you go with him.

(*OFFICER STEWART and the M.C. go into the dressing room and come right out.*)

M.C. Cindy's black boa is gone.

OFFICER STEWART. I'm going to go finish up in the office. (*Exits stage right to the office.*)

CHUCK. (*Whispering to Nick.*) Hey, didn't he say that there were four dead bodies?

NICK. Yeah.

CHUCK. OK, there are three out here and Mike's in the dressing room.

NICK. Yeah?

CHUCK. So where's Cindy?

NICK. That's right.

CHUCK. And, if the scream and the crash we heard before the cops got here wasn't Cindy, who was it, and where is Cindy?

NICK. Good question—both of them.

(M.C. and SANDY enter.)

SANDY. Officer Stewart said we could go home.

OFFICER BRADY. OK, if he's finished getting your statements, then you're done here.

SANDY. *(Seeing the jack-in-the box on the floor.)* Jack Attack!

OFFICER BRADY. I beg your pardon.

SANDY. That's Jack Attack—Mike Thompson's sidekick.

OFFICER BRADY. What are you talking about?

SANDY. This is the jack-in-the-box that Mike Thompson used in his act when he worked here. What's it doing here? *(Starts to go over to the jack-in-the-box.)*

OFFICER BRADY. Stay away from there, Ma'am. Are you sure this is the same jack-in-the-box?

SANDY. Positive. I watched his show every night.

OFFICER BRADY. Interesting. Why don't you go on home now?

SANDY. Where's Mike?

OFFICER BRADY. Go home, please. *(To M.C.)* Both of you. We'll call you when we need you.

(SANDY and M.C. exit.
OFFICER STEWART enters leading CINDY who is in handcuffs.)

OFFICER STEWART. I'll take her down to headquarters and book her.

OFFICER BRADY. OK, I'll wait here for homicide.

(OFFICER STEWART and CINDY exit.)

ALL WITNESSES. Book her?

ALISSA. What's going on? Why is she being arrested?

OFFICER BRADY. We told you we came down here to investigate a series of robberies. Things have been disappearing from the club for the last six months. This started just a little while after Miss Jacobson started working here. The owner was suspicious of her and asked us to come down tonight and pick up a list of stolen objects that we were to get from the M.C. Miss Jacobson saw us coming up the stairs as she was leaving the stage and tried to run out.

ALISSA. What was the crash and scream we heard?

OFFICER BRADY. When she saw us, she was trying to sneak out with a case of champagne. She dropped it and tripped over it. We apprehended her and took her around the back to the office with the rest of the staff for questioning. So, we solved one crime tonight, but now we've got four more on our hands.

(One POLICEMAN [Officer Von Morze] and one POLICE WOMAN [Officer Benson] enter from stage left.)

OFFICER VON MORZE. Officer Brady?

OFFICER BRADY. Yes?

OFFICER VON MORZE. We're from homicide.

OFFICER BRADY. Great. I'm sure you have a lot of questions to ask, so let's get started.

OFFICER VON MORZE. Officer Brady, why don't you question these two women over here *(Alissa and*

Tracie), Officer Benson, you take these two over here
(Chuck and Nick), and I'll take this gentleman right here
(John).

*(The POLICE OFFICERS go to the people assigned to
them and begin questioning them.)*

OFFICER VON MORZE. *(To John.)* Sir, would you
mind waiting over here for me while I rope off the scene of
the crime and outline the bodies?

JOHN. Sure. Do you need any help?

OFFICER VON MORZE. No, thank you. This won't
take long.

OFFICER BENSON. *(To Nick.)* Would you please
wait over there while I talk to this gentleman first?

NICK. You got it. *(Goes to the next table and sits.)*

CHUCK. *(Sits on the table with his feet on the chair.)*
What's your name, officer? What time do you get off duty?
Are you married? Would you like to take a bubble bath?

OFFICER BENSON. I'll ask the questions if you don't
mind. *(Trying not to flirt back.)*

CHUCK. Shoot—so to speak.

OFFICER BENSON. Name?

CHUCK. Chuck O'Donnley. 555-8289.

OFFICER BENSON. *(Half smiling.)* Just answer the
questions.

*(CHUCK looks at the piece of paper to see what she wrote
down and smiles.)*

OFFICER BRADY. *(To Alissa.)* OK, now just relax
and answer the questions as simply as you can. Name?

ALISSA. Alissa Pinkerton.

OFFICER BRADY. What was your relationship to the deceased?

ALISSA. We were friends.

OFFICER BRADY. From your reaction to his death, I'd say you were very good friends. How well did you know him?

ALISSA. (*Composing herself.*) Fairly well.

OFFICER BRADY. Then maybe you can tell me why he was wearing Miss Jacobson's feather boa.

(At this point, there is a moment of silence in the room. EVERYONE heard the question and stops and looks at Alissa to listen to her answer.)

ALISSA. He's a Director at a theater in San Francisco.

(Pause.)

EVERYONE. Oh. (*As if to say, "That explains it."*)

ALISSA. (*To everyone in the room.*) No, you've got it all wrong. He's totally normal. It's just that Cindy had stolen this boa from Dave's theater and he wanted to get it back, so he went in and took it and put it around his neck to hide it until we left, that's all.

OFFICER BRADY. Why didn't he put it in a bag?

ALISSA. He didn't have one.

(EVERYONE goes back to their individual discussions. JOHN notices OFFICER VON MORZE having a hard time drawing the chalk outline of the crime scene and walks over to him.)

JOHN. Hey, Rembrandt, want some help?

OFFICER VON MORZE. I can do this. Just give me another minute.

JOHN. What's the problem?

OFFICER VON MORZE. Look at this. How are we going to tell who's who? This chalk drawing is going to look like some kind of alien creature with three heads and arms and legs all over the place.

JOHN. We can't move them, huh?

OFFICER VON MORZE. No. We've got to keep them exactly the way they are.

JOHN. Well now, wait a minute. You got an eraser in that bag?

OFFICER VON MORZE. No.

JOHN. OK we'll use this. (*HE takes a table cloth off one of the tables and wipes the chalk marks off the floor with it.*) Here, give me that chalk. Now, if we start over here and come around like this, this head could look like boobs belonging to the head on the bottom if we drew the head on the bottom like a side view. You've got him looking straight up. His head's kind of to the side. Just draw it a little more this way. There. Then this arm could look like it goes with this body and this hand would just look like a big flower on his jacket or something.

OFFICER VON MORZE. But he still has three legs.

JOHN. We could get real creative with that.

OFFICER VON MORZE. Give me that chalk! This is a homicide investigation, not "Win, Place or Draw!" (*HE redraws the outline.*) Hand me that ribbon over there.

(JOHN picks up the yellow ribbon and hands it to Officer Von Morze.)

OFFICER VON MORZE. OK, hold this up right here. Now, I'm going to take it over to this wall and tape it, then to the wall in the hallway, then around the dressing room and back to you again. So stay there.

(JOHN holds up the ribbon as OFFICER VON MORZE tapes it by the door leading to the bathroom, and then goes into the hallway. JOHN waits for about thirty seconds and then realizes that HE doesn't have to continue holding it. HE takes gum out of his mouth and fastens his end of the ribbon to the wall with the gum. Then HE ducks under the ribbon and goes into the hallway.)

JOHN. How you doing in here?

(JOHN screams and then frantically jumps over the ribbon back into the lounge. EVERYBODY comes over to him.)

OFFICER BENSON. What happened?
JOHN. There's a snake back there! A huge, ugly, killer of a snake.
TRACIE. Franklin!
OFFICER BRADY. You know this snake?
TRACIE. He's not mine.
OFFICER BRADY. Whose is he?
TRACIE. He's Donna's.

OFFICER BRADY. This Donna's? (*Pointing to the bodies.*)

TRACIE. Yeah.

OFFICER BRADY. Would you mind telling me why this woman brought a snake to a cabaret show with her?

TRACIE. It was a surprise for that Cindy, sort of.

OFFICER BRADY. The singer, Cindy Jacobson?

TRACIE. Yeah.

OFFICER BRADY. Your cousin, Donna, was going to surprise Miss Jacobson with a snake?

TRACIE. Uh huh.

OFFICER BRADY. Do you know why?

TRACIE. I'm not sure, but I think it had something to do with her act.

CHUCK. This I gotta hear.

OFFICER BENSON. (*To Chuck.*) Come on, let's get back to what we were doing. Now, you go over there where your friend is. (*To Nick.*) Could you come over here please?

CHUCK. Will I see you again?

OFFICER BENSON. Count on it.

(*CHUCK and NICK trade places. JOHN goes over and sits with Chuck.*)

OFFICER BENSON. What is your name, sir?

NICK. Nick Hamilton.

OFFICER BENSON. Why did you three come here tonight?

NICK. As you know, Mike used to work here. He just came to visit some of his old friends.

OFFICER BENSON. Mr. O'Donnley said you weren't friends of his.

NICK. That's right.

OFFICER BENSON. If you aren't friends of his, why were you with him?

NICK. We needed to talk to him about a job.

OFFICER BENSON. What kind of job?

NICK. We're both carpenters, and Mike had called us about building a boat house for him.

OFFICER BENSON. Why did he bring his jack-in-the-box with him tonight, and why does it smell like gas?

(NICK shakes his head and shrugs his shoulders.)

OFFICER BRADY. *(To Tracie.)* Why don't you wait over here with these two gentlemen while I talk to this woman *(Alissa)* for a while.

TRACIE. Yeah, sure. *(Goes and sits with Chuck and John.)* So what are yous guys doing here tonight?

CHUCK. My friend, Nick, and I just came in to talk business with this guy.

JOHN. I just came in for a drink with a friend—a client.

TRACIE. Hey, don't bullshit me. I mean, I don't know what's going on here, but this is one hell of a mess we all got here, you know? I mean, four people are dead and no one seems to know anything about it. And you know what that means?

JOHN. What?

TRACIE. Somebody's lying. *(Pause.)* OK, what time did you and your girlfriend get here?

JOHN. She's not my girlfriend. She's my client. She *was* my client.

TRACIE. Whatever!

JOHN. Why should I tell you anything anyway? You're not a cop.

TRACIE. Just work with me on this, OK. Humor me a little. Look at it this way. We're just killing time here.

CHUCK. Bad choice of words.

TRACIE. Yeah, right. So what's your story?

CHUCK. Me and Nick came down to talk to this guy, Mike, about a job.

TRACIE. Yeah, yeah, yeah—everybody's got a story. I think that cop's right. All these dead people got something in common.

CHUCK. Yeah, they're all dead.

TRACIE. Besides that. They all died inside or just outside of Cindy's dressing room and in very weird ways. I think they all knew Cindy and were all in her dressing room for some reason.

JOHN. Hey, uh, shut up, OK?

TRACIE. Oh, did I say something wrong?

CHUCK. Sounds to me like you might have said something right.

TRACIE. Yeah—(*To John.*) So what are you hiding?

JOHN. Nothing—just shut up.

TRACIE. Just don't feel like talking, huh?

CHUCK. (*In a German accent.*) We have ways of making you talk.

JOHN. Hey, both of you shut up and leave me alone. I don't have to talk to you or the cops.

CHUCK. (*Makes a noise like a buzzer.*) Wrong! You're gonna definitely have to talk to the cops, so why don't you practice on us. It might make you relax a little to tell us what happened first.

JOHN. I don't need to relax.

CHUCK. I think you do.

JOHN. Why do you say that?

CHUCK. Because there's a little bitty sweat ball making it's way down the middle of your forehead right now.

JOHN. (*Wipes his forehead.*) Look, just leave me alone, OK? Wait, what about you? What are you hiding?

CHUCK. Nothing. I don't know anything. I don't even know the guy we came to meet.

JOHN. Yeah, right. You and your friend just came here to talk to this guy about a job.

CHUCK. That's right.

JOHN. Then how come the guy you came to talk to is dead?

CHUCK. Wrong place at the wrong time?

TRACIE. Yeah, and what was he doing sitting at the singer's dressing table?

CHUCK. It used to be his dressing table. He used to work here.

JOHN. When?

CHUCK. Just before Cindy.

TRACIE. Oh, so they canned him to hire her, huh?

CHUCK. Yeah, something like that.

TRACIE. (*To John.*) Are you thinking what I'm thinking?

JOHN. Yep. Sounds to me like a good motive for murder.

CHUCK. Look, just shut up, OK—both of you.

TRACIE. Oh, now look who's getting touchy.

CHUCK. (*To Tracie.*) Wait a minute. What about you?

JOHN. Yeah, what's your story? You're so interested in everybody else. What are you doing here?

TRACIE. My cousin and I just came here for a drink.

JOHN. Why this particular bar?

TRACIE. No reason. We were just driving around and got thirsty.

JOHN. Don't tell me she got hit with a bow and arrow in the bathroom.

TRACIE. I don't know. Maybe there's some lunatic Indian running around.

CHUCK. And what about that snake? You seemed to be pretty familiar with him too.

JOHN. Yeah, what about that snake?

TRACIE. Just shut up about him, OK?

JOHN. Oh, so now we have to shut up.

TRACIE. Yeah, both of you!

CHUCK. Hey, I didn't say anything. Don't tell me to shut up!

TRACIE. Well, I'm telling you—shut up!

(Said simultaneously:)

CHUCK.	JOHN.
Don't tell me to shut up! You're the one causing all the trouble playing detective.	You started it! If you hadn't opened your big mouth in the beginning, this wouldn't be happening.

TRACIE. I'm just trying to pass some time here. You don't have to get so jumpy.

OFFICER BRADY. (*Comes over to their table.*) Hey, hey, what's going on over here? If you three can't act like adults, I'm going to have to separate you! Now, everybody just sit down and be quiet.

TRACIE. Hey, Officer, wait a minute. I think I figured this whole thing out. All the dead people knew Cindy, and she's the one that was supposed to die.

OFFICER BRADY. (*Thinks about what Tracie just said.*) I knew that. (*Pause.*) OK, now all of you just sit down and wait here. (*HE signals to OFFICER BENSON to follow him and leads her over to Officer Von Morze.*) I think I just figured this whole thing out. All the dead people knew Cindy, and she's the one that was supposed to die.

OFFICER BENSON. You know, you just might have something there.

OFFICER VON MORZE. You just might. That's very good thinking. We could use someone like you in homicide.

OFFICER BRADY. Thanks.

OFFICER STEWART. (*Enters from stage left, out of breath.*) I left my notes from the interviews here. (*OFFICER STEWART exits stage right to the office, gets his notes and returns to the stage.*) I couldn't believe it. I got half way to the station and realized that I left all my paperwork here.

OFFICER VON MORZE. Wait a minute. You got half way to the station?

OFFICER STEWART. Yeah—pretty bad, huh?

OFFICER VON MORZE. Officer Stewart, if you never got to the station, that means that you still have the suspect with you, or did you lose her too?

OFFICER STEWART. Of course not. She's in the car.

OFFICER VON MORZE. You left a suspect in the car alone?

OFFICER STEWART. Don't worry. She'll be all right. I cracked the window for her.

OFFICER VON MORZE. Did you leave the radio on for her so she can listen to music while you were gone?

OFFICER STEWART. No. I told her I'd be right back.

OFFICER VON MORZE. You moron! She's half way across town by now!

OFFICER STEWART. No she's not. I locked the doors.

OFFICER VON MORZE. I don't believe this!

OFFICER STEWART. Besides, she couldn't get out anyway. I handcuffed her to the steering wheel.

OFFICER VON MORZE. Go get her.

OFFICER STEWART. What?

OFFICER VON MORZE. Go get her. There have been some new developments here since you left, and she may be able to help us.

(OFFICER STEWART exits stage left.)

OFFICER BRADY. Maybe Miss Jacobson will be able to figure out who in this room, dead or alive, would want to kill her.

OFFICER BENSON. I'm going to call the Humane Society and have them come and get this snake.

TRACIE. No! That's Donna's snake, Franklin.

OFFICER BENSON. So the snake's name is Franklin?

TRACIE. Yeah. Franklin Delano Priestly.

OFFICER BENSON. Well, is there somebody Donna would have liked to have take care of her snake for her now?

TRACIE. No, I don't want him. I hate feeding him. Call the Humane Society.

OFFICER BENSON. (*To Officer Brady.*) I'll take care of it.

(*OFFICER BENSON exits stage right. OFFICER STEWART and CINDY enter stage left. CINDY is wearing handcuffs.*)

OFFICER VON MORZE. (*To Officer Stewart.*) Take the cuffs off.

(*OFFICER STEWART takes the handcuffs off Cindy.*)

OFFICER BRADY. Miss Jacobson, do you recognize any of these people.

CINDY. (*Barely looks at the witnesses.*) No. Why? Should I?

OFFICER BRADY. How about these people? (*Leads her over to the dead people.*)

CINDY. (*Bends down and looks at Donna.*) This top one looks familiar, but I'm not positive.

TRACIE. Picture her about fifteen years younger, with acne, a nose like Karl Malden, and about one hundred more pounds.

CINDY. (*Studies Donna for a minute.*) Blubber Lover!

OFFICER BRADY. I beg your pardon?

CINDY. Blubber Lover, Obesity Bong, I could go on. I went to high school with her. I used to have a blast making up all kinds of names for her.

OFFICER BRADY. Real nice. What about the next one?

CINDY. (*Stoops further and looks at Dave.*) Oh, my God! It's Dave Anderson!

OFFICER BRADY. How do you know him?

CINDY. There has only been one man I've ever wanted that I didn't get, and this is him.

ALISSA. What do you mean, you didn't get him?

CINDY. Alissa! You dyed your hair! So he's still screwing you, huh? Does his wife know?

ALISSA. Why you . . . (*Starts after Cindy, but OFFICER BENSON stops her.*) He couldn't stand you, and you tormented him for over two years!

CINDY. Hey, I'm no one-nighter. He insulted me! Nobody screws Cindy Jacobson and doesn't want more!

(*CHUCK looks at Cindy and sits up, as if at attention.*)

OFFICER BRADY. (*To Cindy, pointing to the bodies.*) Continue, please.

CINDY. Now, who do we have here? (*Kneels on the floor to look at Jackie.*) Well, I'll be damned!

TRACIE. No doubt.

CINDY. This is the bitch whose dog almost ruined my car.

JOHN. Hey, have some respect for the dead!

CINDY. (*Looks at John.*) And here's her pea brain lawyer!

JOHN. Her insurance company never should have paid for your car.

CINDY. That damn dog did over fifteen hundred dollars worth of damage to my car!

OFFICER BRADY. All right, all right! There's one more body I want you to look at.

(OFFICER BRADY leads CINDY into the dressing room. After about thirty seconds, THEY come back out.)

CINDY. *(To everyone.)* Well, I'm four for four.

OFFICER BRADY. Sounds to me like they each had a good reason to hate you.

CINDY. Join the club.

OFFICER VON MORZE. Well, this certainly shed some light on the situation. *(To the witnesses.)* You're no longer our star witnesses. You have just graduated to suspects.

ALISSA. Suspects? What for?

OFFICER VON MORZE. Accessory to murder—attempted murder, but what the hell. The way it looks to me is that your friends here *(Pointing to the bodies.)* each snuck into Miss Jacobson's dressing room some time during her performance and set up a deadly trap meant to kill her. However, she never got to her dressing room at intermission, and as they always do, the murderers each returned to the scene of the crime. And, as justice would have it, they each were killed by one of the traps that were set.

CINDY. Boy, what a bunch of neurotic, sadistic assholes! Why can't people just live and let live, like I do?

OFFICER BRADY. Well, I guess that just about wraps this one up.

OFFICER BENSON. Sure does. Boy, what a night. We started out with one suspect and one crime.

OFFICER VON MORZE. Yeah, now we've got . . . (*Points to each suspect and the bodies and counts silently.*) ten suspects and ten crimes. Might as well start cleaning this mess up.

ALISSA. So, Miss Cindy Jacobson, it looks like for once in your life things are not going to go your way. You're finally going to have to pay for at least one wrong thing you've done. That's one good thing that came out of all of this. You always screw things up for everyone else and then come out smelling like a rose. Well, not this time, baby!

NICK. That's right. We'll probably all go to jail, but at least we know that you'll be there too.

CINDY. (*To Officer Von Morze.*) Officer, if I turn states evidence against all these people and promise to return everything I took from the Lounge, could I possibly be granted clemency?

OFFICER VON MORZE. I don't see why not.

CINDY. Of course, I might lose my job.

JOHN. Might lose your job? You've been stealing from your boss. You think they're not going to fire you for that?

TRACIE. That's right, bitch! At least you'll lose your job.

CINDY. I don't want to lose my job. This is the best gig I've ever had. Besides, I'm broke. If I lose my job, I won't be able to pay my rent, and I'll be out on the streets! I don't even have any friends to stay with.

(EVERYONE claps and cheers.)

CINDY. *(Starts to cry.)* I know I haven't exactly been the nicest person in the world, but did it have to come to this?

EVERYONE. Yes!

CINDY. Do I really deserve to end up not only friendless, but homeless, jobless, and broke?

EVERYONE. Yes!

(A MAN wearing a suit and carrying a bunch of red roses enters.)

MAN. Excuse me. I'm looking for a Miss Cindy Jacobson.

CINDY. I'm Cindy Jacobson.

MAN. Well, am I glad to see you. Miss Cindy Jacobson, we've been looking all over for you. *(Yells to offstage left.)* Come on in. She's here.

(TWO MEN walk in holding a giant check for $10,000,000.00.)

MAN. We're from Publishers Clearing House.

END OF PLAY

PROPERTY LIST

Cross-Bow
Bag (large enough for cross-bow)
Bag containing yellow ribbon with "crime scene" written
    on it
Black feather boa with silver sparkles
Chalk
Coat with collar
Donut
Giant check for $10,000,000
Glasses (9)
Handcuffs with key
Jack-in-the-box
Large brown paper bag
Large purse (2)
Notebooks (3)
Pens (3)
Red Roses
Rubber gloves
Stool
Tray for drinks
Waitress order pad